7-

A Week on
Granddaddy's Farm

A Week on Granddaddy's Farm

Millie visits her grandparents on their farm in West Virginia

A Children's Novel

Gail Popp

Gail Popp

Library of Congress Control Number: 2008907593
ISBN: Hardcover   978-1-4363-6588-8
                 Softcover   978-1-4363-6587-1

This is the work of fiction. The incidents are the product of the author's imagination.

This book was printed in the United States of America.

To order additional copies of this book, contact:
Xlibris Corporation
1-888-795-4274
www.Xlibris.com
Orders@Xlibris.com
52583

Table of Contents

For my

grandchildren and great-grandchildren
Aaron, Sara, Dylan, Quinn, and Maya

Acknowledgments

I would like to thank my immediate family and friends who encouraged me and took time to read and critique the chapters during the original writing.

I especially want to thank Susie and Rachel Reddish, my nieces, for their helpful suggestions. Also a special thank you to all my extended family of cousins, aunts, uncles, and grandparents for a lifetime of enduring and enriching memories.

Chapter 1

Grandmother and Granddaddy Boggs and Aunt Susie

It was a lovely July Monday morning in the lush green valley among the West Virginia Appalachian hills on the farm where Millie lived with her parents and four siblings. A late fog hung like a fine cheesecloth curtain over the meadow that lay before the barn, and a gentle creek flowed between the meadow and the country road. A footbridge crossed the creek. "I'm going to Grandmother and Granddaddy Boggs's house for a week," Millie reported excitedly to her sisters, Mae and Belle. "Curtis Lee will be there too!" It was going to be lots of fun. In her eight years, Millie had stayed for a week only once before.

"Remember, Millie, you're not going as a guest. You're a member of the family, and you have to help Grandmother and Aunt Susie every day," Mom reminded her. Millie's mother was preparing to go to the general store and Looneyville Post Office where she was the postmaster and sole proprietor with her husband. They had constructed the building that housed the store and post office; and Millie's mother, Rebecca, worked there six days a week. The little building with its cement porch and steps stood by the dirt road with its flagpole and single gas pump to the right of the building. Mail carriers met at the post office to receive mail from the carrier who brought it by truck from Spencer, a small town about an hour drive from Looneyville. As Millie and her mother walked across the bridge, Millie assured her mother she would be a good helper. "You have to mind, too. Whatever Grandmother or Aunt Susie says you have to do whether you want to or not, right?" Mom wanted everything understood clearly to avoid any problems.

"I always mind, Mom. Honest!" Millie had her suitcase in hand. She was catching a ride with the mailman. It would take about two hours to get to Grandmother and Granddaddy's up on Duck Run near Linden. It would be fun to help Uncle Ward, the mailman, too. He drove a jeep with no doors, and Millie handed him the mail. Sometimes he'd let her put it in the mailbox, especially if it were a hard box to reach from the jeep.

"Give me a kiss and be good," instructed Mom as Uncle Ward neatly stacked the mail he had sorted into piles and placed them in the order they were to be delivered in his jeep.

"Let me put that suitcase in the back and we'll be off," Uncle Ward said. Millie and Uncle Ward talked about the people they knew, the animals they had, the weather, and the interesting stops the open-air jeep made at mailboxes. Time fairly flew, and before Millie realized it, she was at the bottom of the hill at Grandmother Boggs's place.

Granddaddy sat on the vine-covered porch in his cane rocking chair. He was leaning forward, peering intently. "Is that you, Millie?" He called to her in his strong preacher voice.

"Yep! It's me, Granddaddy!" Millie called back excitedly. She jumped from the jeep and ran to the back to get her suitcase. "Seems you've got a new boarder here, Poppy!" Uncle Ward joked loudly as he climbed back into his jeep.

"I hope she doesn't eat us out of house and home!" Granddaddy joked back. Uncle Ward told Millie he'd pick her up next week if she wanted to go back with him. Millie carried her suitcase up the steep hill to the little unpainted house at the top of the hill. Aunt Susie in her long cotton housedress, bibbed apron, and sunbonnet came limping around the side of the house to meet Millie. She had rheumatoid arthritis in her hip, and it caused her to limp when she walked. Her arms were outstretched to receive a hug. Granddaddy held the bowl of his pipe in his hand and waited in his chair for his hug. The sweet aroma of tobacco surrounded him, and the blooming honeysuckle fragrance was all around. His Santa Claus beard was soft and loving against Millie's face, and his big arms enveloped her in his hug.

In the house, she found Grandmother standing in the kitchen at the woodburning cookstove in her long cotton housedress and bibbed apron, fixing lunch. She turned from the stove for her hug and then back to stirring the July applesauce. The pleasant scent of apples and woodsmoke mingled in the air. Everything looked the same to Millie. She carried her suitcase up the steep narrow stairs to Aunt Susie's room. She knew that was where she'd sleep. The upstairs slanting ceiling seemed to add to the closeness of the room. At one end was the window that looked out on the yard and barn lot. At the other end of the room were the stairs, and beyond that the spare bedroom. Aunt Susie's room had a big four-poster steel bed, a dresser with mirror, a chair, a folding screen, and a clothespress. Millie always slept with Aunt Susie. "Millie, come out here and talk to me!" Granddaddy demanded from his porch chair. He had been a preacher before he got sick and had to quit. One of his legs was folded back, locked at the knee, and he could only walk with crutches. He always wore a white shirt, a black suit coat, and black pants. His long white beard and hair contrasted his ruddy complexion. His strongest features were his eyes. His clear hazel gaze could frighten or twinkle with merriment. He never missed a chance to preach, especially to his grandchildren. "Now, tell me, Millie, have you been saying your prayers?" he demanded in his loud preacher voice.

"Yes, Granddaddy. Every night!" Millie replied honestly. She sat across from him on the porch in a homemade cane-bottomed chair, her eyes sparkling with excitement.

"Well now, you know you don't have to wait until night to say a prayer. You know that, don't you?" Granddaddy liked to talk about the Lord and the Bible.

"Yes, I know. I can say a prayer anytime, anywhere," Millie replied.

"Right!" Granddaddy shouted. He slapped his hand on his knee and stamped his good foot on the porch floor to celebrate her correct answer. "Now, you go help your grandmother and we'll talk some more later." "OK, Granddaddy." Millie liked talking to Granddaddy about religion. Some of the grandchildren were only polite, but Millie found their conversations interesting and stimulating, and she loved his stories. Aunt Susie had gone to pick green beans in the garden below the hill, and Grandmother was still in the kitchen. "Can I help you, Grandmother?"

"You can set the table, Millie," Grandmother replied. "The plates are in the corner safe. Do you know how many you'll need?" Grandmother was not a large woman, but in her long dress and bibbed apron with the pocket in the front, she was impressive. Her long gray hair was rolled up and held in place with side combs and large bobby pins. She had had thirteen children and raised ten to adulthood. Millie's mother was next to Aunt Susie who was the oldest. Three of her children had died as babies.

"We'll need four—one for you, Granddaddy, Aunt Susie, and me," Millie said as she counted out the plates.

"And one more for Curtis Lee," Grandmother said with a smile.

"Curtis Lee's coming to eat?" she asked in surprise. She thought that maybe tomorrow she'd see her cousin. They had great fun together. He just lived up the road a ways.

"Yes, he knew you were coming with the mail today so he's planning to come to see you as soon as his morning chores are done. He should be here anytime now." Grandmother emptied the freshly cooked July apples into a vegetable dish. Millie carried it from the kitchen to the dining room table. A large wood cookstove dominated the old-fashioned kitchen. It stood about a foot from the wall, and behind it were the woodbox, a stoker, and work gloves. It was a wonderful stove, Millie thought. It had a warming oven across the top, a large cooking oven underneath, a water tank along the side, and burner covers that lifted off for putting in the wood. Grandmother did most of the cooking in the morning while it was cool. She knew just the right-sized fire to make and how to bank the coals to keep the fire alive without heating up the house. Food had a different flavor when cooked on the woodstove, more natural somehow. Lunchtime was called dinner, and it was the biggest meal of the day. Grandmother was fixing chicken and dumplings (one of her specialties), applesauce, corn on the cob, green beans, coleslaw, sliced tomatoes, and as always, corn bread, butter, and milk.

On the other side of the kitchen was a storage cabinet with counter space for making pies or washing dishes in dishpans. There was no running water or sink in Grandmother's kitchen. The well pump was in the backyard. If the water bucket, which sat on the counter, became empty, Millie knew it was her job to fill it. The hot-water tank on the woodstove was kept full too. Millie checked the water bucket and it was full. "Do you need some wood brought in for the stove, Grandmother?" Millie inquired, noticing the few sticks of kindling in the woodbox.

"Yes, Millie, we could use some more wood. Do you remember where the woodpile is?"

"Down at the bottom of the hill?"

"Yes, get the wood beside the tin sheet. It's the driest," Grandmother directed.

"OK." Millie dashed out the back door, through the fence gate, and down the hill to the woodpile. She could see Aunt Susie, red-faced in her sunbonnet and long dress and apron, coming toward the house from the garden with a basket over her arm. Corn ears were sticking up over the edge. "I'm getting some wood, Aunt Susie," she announced.

"Good for you, Millie! We always need wood carried up to the house." Aunt Susie continued up the steep hill toward the house.

Suddenly, down the hill ran Curtis Lee. His face was beaming with anticipation when Millie looked up and saw him. "Hi, Millie!" Curtis shouted. "I heard you were coming today!" He was about the same size as Millie, and they were about the same age. Both children were dressed in jeans, T-shirts, and tennis shoes. Curtis Lee's brown hair was cut short all over, and his sparkling brown eyes and big smile showed his excitement. Millie's hair was short and blond, and she had hazel eyes, otherwise they might have been mistaken for brother and sister.

"I know. Grandmother told me. I'm glad. Want to help me get wood for the stove?" Millie was placing sticks of wood in her arms from the pile as Grandmother had instructed.

"Sure." Curtis Lee started pulling wood sticks from the woodpile and laying them across his arm as Millie was doing. With their arms full, they trudged up the hill carefully so as not to drop their heavy load of wood. Aunt Susie was waiting at the top of the hill.

"You children are a big help to me," Aunt Susie said. "That's more than enough wood. I don't want you to wear yourselves out." Her smile and friendly manner were encouraging to the children. They assured their aunt that they were strong and not a bit tired. "When we get in the house, we'll help you string the beans too," Millie told Aunt Susie, and Curtis Lee agreed.

"Good! I need some good bean stringers. You wash your hands at the pump, and I'll get us some pans," Aunt Susie told them. Curtis Lee and

Millie deposited their load in the woodbox behind the stove and went directly to the pump to wash their hands.

"I'll pump first, Millie, OK?" Curtis Lee liked to think of himself as bigger and older, even though he was only a few months older than Millie and a few inches taller. They took turns washing at the pump and dried their hands on the towel at the washstand that stood along the wall beside the house. They each got a drink of cool well water from the tin cup that hung on the pump.

Aunt Susie had a chair and three pans with the bean basket. She washed the beans and gave each child a few to string in a pan. The children sat on the grass in the shade. It was always more fun to string beans at Grandmother's than at home. Here it was fun! They talked, laughed, told jokes, and soon the beans were all gone, and they helped shuck the corn ears and threw the shucks into the pigpen.

"You go see your granddad, Curtis Lee, and you too, Millie, while your grandmother and I finish dinner. We'll call you when it's ready. You're really good helpers. Thank you," Aunt Susie called as she went in the kitchen door.

"Come on, Millie," Curtis Lee said. They walked around the side of the house and passed Grandmother's flowers and her favorite snowball bush to where Granddaddy sat on the porch smoking his pipe and reading his Bible. Ivy and honeysuckle vines grew along the side of the porch and up the porch railing. Granddaddy had a small table beside his handmade rocking chair that held his Prince Albert tobacco can, paper, and pencils. Several chairs lined the wall of the porch on either side of Granddaddy's chair. A wooden swing hung from the porch ceiling on the end opposite the stone steps. "Hi, Granddaddy," Curtis Lee said as they climbed the stone steps onto the porch. "How are you today?"

"Well, if it's not Curtis Lee!" declared Granddaddy. "Come to see us, did you?" He held his pipe bowl as he talked and laid his well-worn Bible on the table beside his chair.

"Yep, I came to spend the day!" Curtis announced as he and Millie climbed up the steps to the porch and sat down in the swing.

"That's good! Now, tell me, what are you two scalawags up to?" Granddaddy always called them scalawags, whatever that was. His eyes were atwinkle, and he leaned forward in his chair to peer at the children.

"We're going to go see the horses after dinner, Granddaddy, and maybe we'll go up the creek and look for stuff," Curtis Lee explained.

"Oh, I see. You're going exploring, are you? Just like Lewis and Clark, eh?"

"Who's that?" asked Millie.

"You never heard of Lewis and Clark?" Granddaddy stormed in amazement.

"Nope," the children responded. Granddaddy told them about the two great explorers who blazed new trails in the wilderness. His story was exciting, filled with many accents and flares of waving arms, foot stamps, and clouds of smoke from his pipe. Wild animals, terrible weather, savage redskins, and one Indian woman who helped guide the explorers and probably saved their lives. He told of men of courage and daring and kept the children enthralled until Aunt Susie called them to dinner.

Granddaddy offered the blessing and then the food was passed around the dining room table. Everything was so good, Millie decided. "No one cooks like you do, Grandmother!" she said. The meal was pleasant and filling. Millie and Curtis Lee remembered their manners and asked to help with the dishes, but Grandmother said for them to go play but to be back before supper.

"You explorers keep your eyes open out there for treasures. You never know what you might find," Granddaddy reminded them as they ran out the kitchen door.

"We will," they called back.

Millie

Chapter 2

Treasure Hunting

The horses were in the field across the road. They spied Molly, Grandmother's favorite, a gray mare. She was grazing in the shadow of the hillside. Beside her was Duke, the brown saddle horse that was Aunt Susie's. There standing by itself was the new horse. It was bronze-colored with a white star on its face and white hair above its hoofs.

"Ain't she pretty?" Curtis Lee said admiringly. "Her name's Boots. Can you see why?" They were leaning against the wire fence that enclosed the field and looking through the holes in the wire.

"Yeah. I see her white feet," Millie said. "Is she gentle? Can you ride her?"

"I haven't ridden her yet, but Aunt Susie said when you came she'd let us ride her. Maybe tomorrow."

"Oh good! I can hardly wait!" The only time Millie had a chance to ride a horse was at Granddaddy Boggs's. She often rode the mules, John and Jerry, but it was always bareback or with a harness on. A horse was different and with a saddle too! That would be a treat.

They turned from the fence surrounding the field and started along the creek bed that followed the road to Curtis Lee's house.

"Ain't Granddaddy funny," Curtis Lee said. "I wish I lived in the days of Lewis and Clark!"

"Me too. Granddaddy's really a good storyteller. I like to hear about when he used to be a preacher and traveled from church to church on his big black stallion. Do you remember any of those stories?" Millie had picked up a walking stick, and she leaned on it as she walked, pretending to have a sore leg.

"Yeah, like the time a panther jumped on his horse's back in that wilderness ride and almost got him." Millie had not heard of that story. Curtis Lee had found a stick and he too leaned on it, walking with one stiff leg along the dry rocky creek bed or used it to swipe at touch-me-not flowers. He spied a shiny metallic rock in the stream that flowed in a low place where water had pooled. It hadn't rained for over a week, and the wet weather creek bed was nearly dry. "Hey, look what I found!"

"What is it?" Millie came to see what Curtis Lee was looking at among the gravel and rocks, which lay on the wet creek bed.

"See!" He picked up a rock with gold color specks in it, and they examined it closely together.

"What is it?" Millie asked again. She squinted her eyes for a clearer look.

"Maybe it's gold!" Curtis Lee said excitedly. He was holding the shiny rock in his hand, turning it over and over.

"Nah, there's no gold around here," Millie decided.

"How do you know? There might be!" declared Curtis Lee. "Let's go show Granddaddy!" The children dropped their sticks and ran back to the porch where Granddaddy sat smoking his pipe and reading his Bible.

"Granddaddy, guess what? We found gold!" Curtis Lee announced. He was holding the shiny rock in his extended hand for all to see.

"What! Gold, you say! Now, that's really something! You're prospectors, are you? Let me see that gold you say you found." Granddaddy examined it carefully. "Now, this looks like gold all right. But I think you got fooled. I think what you prospectors found is fool's gold."

"What's fool's gold?" Millie wanted to know.

"That's what you've got here. It fooled you, didn't it? When prospectors go prospecting, they get fooled sometimes, and that's what happened to you two. You got fooled with fool's gold." Granddaddy's eyes were dancing, and the children knew he was teasing them.

"Oh," was all they could say, disappointment obvious in their faces.

"But now, see here. That doesn't mean there's not gold down there. You just quit too soon. Where there's fool's gold, there may be *real* gold. Now, here's what you need to do. Go back to where you found this and look again. Take something to put your gold in when you find it, and we'll decide how much it's worth after you get done," Granddaddy spoke seriously. "Look out back there for a coffee can to carry your gold in. Now, off with you!"

"OK, Come on, Millie!" Curtis Lee was full of hope and excitement. "I bet we really do find gold this time!" Millie followed along, but somehow she couldn't quite get into the spirit of prospecting as Curtis Lee did. They searched the creek bed for gold-speckled rocks but found only a few more. As they looked, they found other interesting rocks, small minnows caught in pools, crawl crabs under rocks, bones, and shells to show Granddaddy. Wandering into the hillside woods near the creek, they found a loose grapevine hanging from a tree. They took turns running down the hill holding on to the vine and swinging by their arms. Their feet kicked wildly in the air out over the creek bed and back. Three swings each then it was the other person's turn.

"Let's go up to the Pyramids and play," Millie said as she let go of the vine after many turns on the swing.

"There are copperhead snakes up there. Grandmother said we couldn't go up there without Sam," Curtis Lee replied. The Pyramids was a large rock formation that sat on top of the hill behind the house. The children would have to climb the hill and go through briers, high weeds, and bushes with tangled vines to the path that led to the rocks. The rocks lay one against the other with overhangs and cavelike indentions, nature's sculpture. The land was level around the rocks, a meadow plain atop the hill. It was a strange rock formation that may have been placed there for some strange ancient purpose long ago or, more likely, it was an act of nature created by erosion. Most of the grandchildren liked to climb on it and play cops and robbers or cowboys and Indians there.

"Let's go to your house and get Sam. I have to go to the outhouse anyway," Millie suggested. Sam was Curtis Lee's collie dog and he would scare snakes away if any were there.

"He's not home. He went with my dad this morning to the field," Curtis Lee said.

"I gotta go," Millie insisted as she started back through the woods toward the barnyard. The woods along the creek bordered the barnyard with its assortment of buildings—a chicken house and little shack for setting hens, the barn, the pigpen, and most important of all, the toilet or outhouse. The outhouse was about sixty feet from the yard gate near the top of the hill with a path that connected them, one to the other. Millie stopped to use the toilet while Curtis Lee continued on to the porch to share their treasure with Granddaddy.

Granddaddy looked carefully through the contents of the coffee can, helping the children identify each item—limestone, sandstone, quartz, conglomerate stones, coal clinkers, mussel shells, flint, various small shells, and bones, etc. Aunt Susie brought them each a tall glass of sweetened tea made with cool well water. They sat on the porch talking, sipping tea, and enjoying each other's company. As evening approached, Curtis Lee said goodbye with a promise to return in the morning. Millie and Aunt Susie began the evening chores.

Chapter 3

The Parlor Surprise

It was time to milk the cow. Millie went to the upper field behind the house to get Bossie. She didn't have to go far because Bossie knew it was time to be milked, and she was grazing toward the milking place under the huge apple tree near the yard gate. Aunt Susie had a special milking stool and a special milk bucket. She slipped a rope around Bossie's neck and gave her some grain in a bucket to eat while she was being milked. Five meowing farm cats had gathered around an old cake pan on the ground that served as the feed pan. Aunt Susie poured the pan full of warm foamy white milk, and the cats quickly licked it clean. Their little pink tongues lapped with a *snunk, snunk, snunk* that made Millie laugh. She squatted beside Aunt Susie and talked to the cats as they lapped the milk and waited for more. Together, the cats consumed three pans full and then each walked away to clean its face with a lick of a paw and a wipe on the ear, nose, and mouth, all in one motion. Millie liked cats, but Grandmother and Aunt Susie's cats were all barnyard cats. Grandmother said she couldn't stand cat hairs in the house or cats rubbing against her leg so they were not pets.

After milking was over and Bossie was free to graze in the field again, Aunt Susie and Millie took the bucket of milk to the house. The milk was strained through cheesecloth, placed in crock bowls with lids, and carried to the root cellar to cool. The root cellar was dug under a small hill off the kitchen door near the well pump. Its wooden door was unlatched with a small crossbar, and it had a strong spring at the top to keep it closed.

Inside were shelves from the ceiling to the floor on two sides and bins in the back for potatoes, apples, and other raw vegetables. On the floor were crock bowls with milk, cream, butter, cottage cheese, and buttermilk that needed to be kept cold. The cellar had a cool dry feeling and mixed aromas of vegetables, fruit, and sour milk filled the air.

Supper was light—corn bread and milk, cold chicken, and other leftovers from dinner. After the blessing, they ate together around the dining room table. Mealtime was pleasant and mannerly with conversation drifting back and forth across the table. Everyone was soon finished eating and ready to leave the table.

"Millie, we want to paper the parlor tomorrow. Do you think you and Curtis Lee would like to help?" Aunt Susie asked. Grandmother and Granddaddy listened intently, waiting for Millie's reaction.

"Sure, I'd like to! I help Mom do stuff all the time. We paint or paper at least one room in the house every year."

"Well, the rolls of wallpaper are lying there, and neither Mommy nor I can climb very well. We thought that maybe you and Curtis Lee could climb the ladders for us and put up the high part of the strips. We don't have to worry about matching it," Aunt Susie explained to Millie.

"Don't worry, we can do it. I've seen Mom do it lots of times." Millie was excited at the thought of being the one to really wallpaper a room. She had never done anything more than go get things for people or take things away. She had never been asked to do the important stuff. What a great surprise!

"We'll need to move the furniture into the center of the room tonight so we'll be ready to start early tomorrow before it gets hot," Grandmother said. She had imagined the children would want to help them.

"You didn't know you were going to be a paper hanger, did you?" Granddaddy teased.

"No, but I can. It'll be fun! When do we start?"

"As soon as we clear the table and wash the dishes," Grandmother said cheerfully.

Granddaddy turned in his chair, and leaning on his crutches, he pulled himself to stand on his one good leg. The other leg was drawn back at the knee, frozen in position above the floor. "If it wasn't for this bad leg of mine, I'd be doing it," he said as he hobbled back through the living room to the porch.

"Now, Poppy, you mustn't talk that way!" Aunt Susie scolded. "You have enough to do studying the Bible and writing your lectures. Do you have any ready to send away?"

"Not quite, but soon," he responded from the porch screen door. "Soon."

Aunt Susie and Millie quickly cleared the table and took the dishes to the kitchen. Grandmother had the pans of water ready for washing and rinsing the dishes. Millie took some leftovers to the hogpen and some to the cats' and dog's pans under the apple tree. She called, "Kitty, Kitty, Kitty! Here, Betsy! Here, Betsy!" From the barn, the cats came scampering up the hill. Betsy, the dachshund, appeared from under the house, walking lazily toward Millie. She was Aunt Susie's dog and stayed around the house or followed Aunt Susie, but hid when others came around. She seldom barked and Grandmother said a worthless dog like that was nothing but a nuisance. Aunt Susie said to leave Betsy alone. It was a free country, and she could bark or not bark it didn't matter to her.

After the kitchen was clean, the next task was moving the furniture in the parlor or sitting room as it was sometimes called. It had a large four-poster double bed with a straw tick mattress and a feather comforter. There were two cane-backed cherry chairs—one rocker and one captain's chair with arms and a high back, a small cherry library table, a painted nightstand covered with a decorative throw, and a cabinet Victrola with a handle to wind it up. Pull-down blinds and once-white lace curtains were over the windows. The wallpaper, which had been cream colored with a small pink and green flower design, was now dingy from woodsmoke. It needed papering, all right, Millie decided.

Chapter 4

Remembering

Soon, all the furniture was piled in the center of the room except the bed. It would be taken down the next day. The sun had gone down behind Bailey's farmhouse, which looked like a tiny speck in the distance on top of the hill to the left across Calhoun Road. On the porch, Granddaddy sat smoking his pipe with his small wire-rimmed magnifying glasses low on his nose. He looked off into space, lost in his concentration. From time to time, he wrote in his notebook, his Bible open in his lap. A mist was beginning to gather in the low parts of the valley along Duck Run Road and the creek bed. Three hard rock dirt roads, which followed mountain streams, came together at the bottom of the hill where the mailbox stood. One road to the left led to Calhoun County, and one to the right led to a dead-end hollow where Curtis Lee lived. The two roads merged into one at the base of Granddaddy's hill and continued to follow the creek about two miles to the highway and Linden. Hillsides clean and green towered above the valley on the left below Bailey's house. Horses, sheep, and goats grazed on the hillside. A wood was on both sides of the road to the right. In the mist of evening, the valley was peaceful and quiet, except for the crickets and frogs' music. They were tuning up for their nightly concert. From the porch on the hill, two hilltop farms were barely visible. Bailey's farm was on the left, and Uncle Ward's above the woods on the right. Soon the valley would be dark.

Aunt Susie, Grandmother, and Millie came to sit on the porch with Granddaddy and watch the day fade into night. Aunt Susie and Millie sat on the porch swing, gently swinging, and Grandmother sat beside Granddaddy in a cushioned cane-woven chair. She had a sewing basket in her lap, and from it, she took a crochet hook and yarn and continued the rug she was making.

"I wonder how Mrs. Bailey is," Grandmother said as her fingers worked the crochet hook and yarn.

"She's not much better," Aunt Susie responded. "I talked to Billy on his way to the store when I was picking beans, and he said she was still poorly."

"That's too bad. She's ninety-five you know, and when a person that age gets a cold, it's likely to turn into pneumonia before you know it," Grandmother said, never looking up from her crochet work.

"That reminds me of the time I got pneumonia when I was preaching down in Virginia. Did you hear about that, Millie?" Granddaddy peered at Millie over his wire-rimmed magnifying glasses.

"No, I don't think so." Millie was thoughtful, but couldn't recall the story.

"Well, sir, it was like this. I had been traveling through what is now West Virginia and Virginia organizing churches for the Seventh-Day Adventists. West Virginia was all called Virginia then. I rode on horseback 'cause there weren't any cars in those days. I never took anything with me. Because Jesus said, 'Take no thought for your life, what ye shall eat, or what ye shall drink; nor yet for your body, what ye shall put on. Is not life more than meat, the body then raiment? Behold the fowls of the air: for they sow not, neither do they reap, nor gather into barns; yet your heavenly Father feedeth them. Are ye not much better than they'[Matthew 6:25-26]. Jesus also said, 'Go ye into all the world, and preach the gospel to every creature' [Mark 16:15]. So like the first disciples of old, I went out to places that never had a church and I helped the people organize one.

"At that time, I was called a missionary. I would ride into a settlement and find out the name of the leader there. Then I'd pay a visit to him. He'd give me room and board and arrange for me to preach at a particular time and place. He'd put up posters and send out the word to all the surrounding area, and then I'd stop back in about a month to hold the services. I usually just stayed about two or three days in one place, sometimes just overnight. It all depended on the distance between the settlements.

"Well, sir, this one trip was especially nasty. It had been raining for days, and I had to keep moving, just me and my horse Sampson. He was one fine stallion! My pa gave him to me when I felt the call to go preach the Word of God. He was coal black with a little white spot on his forehead, the most handsome horse in any of these parts. His hair was soft as velvet, and he was strong and I mean strong! He carried me through rain, wind, snow, and the heat of summer. We were together all the years until I got sick and had to quit. But we were friends, you know. Not like one of those horses there." He waved his hand toward the bottom field where the horses grazed. "Anyway, on this certain trip, as I said, it had been raining for days. Sampson and me had some really rough land to travel. It was real wilderness. In those days, there were bear and panthers, wildcats and poison snakes. There weren't many doctors then either. Not like now. People doctored themselves. As I said, Sampson and me had a long way to travel through a rocky mountain pass where there was a very narrow road to follow, hardly big enough for a wagon. There was a wood on one side and a deep ravine on the other, you know, a cliff. If a fellow fell over that cliff, he and his horse were sure goners. Well, Sampson and me had to go along that mountain pass for about five miles. We'd been traveling for two days, and if I figured it right, I knew we'd be at Mr. O'Hara's before dark. I never traveled at night. It was too dangerous, wild animals and all. I was feeling rather poorly, had a bad cold that was getting worse. But I was scheduled to preach on Sunday, and that was Friday. It had stopped raining, but like now, a mist was falling and it was about this time of day, not dark and not light. We started along the pass fine. Sampson was sure-footed, and I never had to worry about him stumbling or falling. I was worried about wild animals that might smell a man and a horse. Sampson was nervous too. I could feel it. We were about three miles along the pass when Sampson began to act odd. He bucked up and refused to go forward. I knew some kind of wild animal was up ahead. I didn't know if it was a wildcat, bear, or what. We couldn't go back. I figured our only chance was to outrun it. So I patted Sampson and talked to him real soft. I had a riding crop and a coiled whip on the side of my saddle that could be used as weapons. I never used mine except if I was in danger, but I knew how to use them. I drove a wagon team for my pa at the logging camp where I got my leg smashed. Somehow, I had to make Sampson run full speed passed whatever was lurking in the woods up ahead.

"Like I said, I figured the only way out was to surprise the varmint and outrun it. So I pulled out my riding crop and I hit Sampson as hard as I could on the rump. He was so startled that he took off like an arrow shot from a bow. Well, sir, I heard a crash, and I felt a weight behind me on Sampson's back and then it was gone. I looked back and a surprised black panther was standing in the road behind us. Poor Sampson's hindquarters were bleeding and raw where the panther had scratched him. We were going so fast that I could hardly stay in the saddle. Before I knew it, we were at Mr. O'Hara's farm, and he was tending to Sampson's wounds and to me too. 'Cause I was so weak, I couldn't walk for a few minutes and Sampson was trembling all over. You ever been that scared, Millie? I doubt it. I was never that scared before or since."

Granddaddy leaned back, and striking a kitchen match on his leg, he drew a deep inhale on his pipe stem while holding the lighted match to the pipe bowl. Everyone was quietly watching as the smoke began to puff from his mouth and the match light flickered and died with an absent flick of the hand. The sweet tobacco aroma drifted across the porch in the evening stillness. Grandmother's fingers were quiet in her lap inside the sewing basket, and Aunt Susie and Millie sat still in the swing. Night came quickly in the hills once the sun was gone, and now, it was more dark than light. "What happened next, Granddaddy?"

"Well, sir, I was sick the next day. Got all fevered in the night. But I preached on Sunday to a big crowd. There were always big crowds in those days 'cause they'd be months without a preacher in the settlements. I was always busy with weddings, funerals, and visits to make besides preaching. By Sunday night, I had the chills and was bedfast for a week. I stayed two weeks at Mr. O'Hara's. I'll be forever grateful to those good people!"

"Praise God!" Grandmother said softly.

"That's really something, Granddaddy!" Millie's eyes were wide in admiration. "You were really brave! Just think—attacked by a panther and you lived to tell about it!"

"It's God's will, child," Grandmother reminded her.

"Come on, Millie. Time for bed," said Aunt Susie. "Let's go visit *Johnny House* out back and then it's up to bed we go. I'll get the lamp. Say good night to your grandmother and granddaddy." Millie obediently planted a big loving kiss on the cheek of each of her grandparents, and then she and Aunt Susie went inside to get the oil lamps, which sat on the dining room bureau. Aunt Susie lifted the globe, and with a turn of the switch, she lighted the wick and then adjusted the flame. She did the same to the larger lamp and took it into the living room so Grandmother and Granddaddy could see when coming in from the porch. She took the little one with her out the back door, across the yard, and through the gate to the outhouse that was on the hillside barnyard. Aunt Susie held the lamp for Millie while she went in and Millie held the lamp for Aunt Susie, and then they returned to the house and upstairs to bed.

"Don't forget, we must say our prayers. What will you say to God in your prayers, Millie?" Aunt Susie asked as she undressed behind the folding screen, which she pulled from along the wall.

"I always say my prayers at night," Millie replied. "Sometimes Mom hears them, but usually, I just say them myself. Will you hear my prayers tonight, Aunt Susie?"

"Yes, as soon as you're ready, you go ahead. I'm listening." It always took Aunt Susie a long time to dress and undress because of her arthritis.

"OK." Millie knelt beside the bed in her pajamas. "Dear Jesus, thank you for letting me come to Grandmother and Granddaddy and Aunt Susie's. Bless Mom, Dad, Belle, Mae, Harry, Marion, old Annie, and all the cats. Help me be good. Amen. How's that?"

"I'm sure God liked your prayer very much, Millie," Aunt Susie said as she came from behind the screen in her light cotton floor-length gown. Her light brown hair, kept in braids wrapped around her head, was down; and she came to sit in front of the dresser mirror to let out the braids and brush her long hair, which hung in crinkly waves to her waist. She brushed in long strokes, pulling her hair in front across her breast, brushing and brushing. The lamplight flickered, making shadows dance around the walls and ceiling. Millie watched the flickering light, dancing shadows, and Aunt Susie brushing her hair over and over in front of the dressing table. The odor of lamp oil smoke was in the air. Soft voices drifted up the stairs from below, and faint night sounds could be heard in the semidarkness. Millie felt cozy and safe and happy, snuggling in Aunt Susie's straw tick bed with a cotton sheet covering her. Tomorrow would be another exciting day.

Granddaddy

Chapter 5

The Paper Hangers

When Millie awoke, she was alone in the bed. It was light, and she could hear movement downstairs. Wonder what time it was? She scrambled out of bed and dashed to the window. Through the misty morning, she could see Aunt Susie milking under the apple tree beyond the fence gate. She searched through her suitcase for clean clothes. She wasn't allowed to bring shorts to Granddaddy's. He didn't like for girls to show their legs because he believed females were ladies and should be covered from head to toe. So she put on clean underwear, jeans, a cotton T-shirt, socks, and tennis shoes; placed her dirty things back along the side of the suitcase; and closed the lid. She straightened the sheets on the bed, brushed her short brown hair quickly, and hurried downstairs.

Granddaddy sat in his cherry handmade rocker beside the living room window where he could see the yard, well pump, cellar door, yard gate, and shady apple tree. A potbellied stove stood in the corner in front of Granddaddy's chair, and a woodbox was beside the stove next to the wall. The cold top of the stove served as a shelf in summer for Granddaddy's odds and ends. Beside his rocker were his crutches and a small cloth-covered table, which held his Prince Albert tobacco can, pipe, well-worn Bible, notebook, and assortment of pencils, pens, and papers. A daybed with cushions and a colorful handmade quilt cover stood along the opposite wall. Various cane-woven cherry chairs were placed about the small living room. Linoleum covered the floors throughout the house. Handmade crocheted throw rugs were beneath the chairs. Because of Granddaddy's crutches, throw rugs were always anchored under furniture. A small end table stood at the end of the daybed, and another small table was under the window that faced the porch. Lightly patterned wallpaper covered the walls, and scenic pictures of faraway places were placed here and there on the walls. A framed sketch of Uncle Sam done by the family artist, Uncle Ronnie, was on the wall above the table by the daybed.

"Morning, Granddaddy," Millie said cheerfully as she bounced into the room.

"Well, what is this coming in? A grasshopper, is it?" He turned to face the bright-eyed child.

"No, just me, Granddaddy." She smiled happily. "How are you today?"

"Me? I couldn't be better! You ready to be a paper hanger?"

"I sure am," she called back as she hopped through the dining room into the kitchen where Grandmother stood before the wood burning cookstove, frying sausages. Coffee aroma prevailed among the sausage and warming applesauce odors. "Morning, Grandmother," she called in passing as she dashed out the back door and through the yard gate toward the outhouse. Mist hung heavy in the cool morning air. "Morning, Aunt Susie," she called.

"Morning, Millie," Aunt Susie responded without looking up. Seated on the three-legged milk stool, her head leaning against the side of the cow, she used both hands to direct two continuous streams of milk into the milk pail. Betsy lay beside Aunt Susie and looked up as Millie dashed past.

After a few minutes, Millie was back, patting Betsy on the head and looking about the hillside barnyard.

"Can I do anything, Aunt Susie?" she asked.

"You can check with your grandmother to see if she needs wood for the woodbox if you want to."

"Sure." Away Millie scurried. Inside, only a few wood sticks remained in the box. "I'm going to get the wood, Grandmother," she reported. And before Grandmother could answer, she was gone again through the gate and down the hill to the woodpile. After loading her arms with wood sticks, she trudged more slowly up the hill with her load. Aunt Susie had finished milking and waited at the gate to open and close it for Millie, a pail of milk in her hand. After washing her hands at the well pump, Millie was ready to help with breakfast. Curtis Lee would be coming soon to help her with the wallpaper.

The table was set for breakfast with eggs, sausage, biscuits and gravy, creamed tomatoes, sliced potatoes fried in butter, coffee, milk, jellies, and butter. Granddaddy said the blessing, and they ate the hearty breakfast in good humor and pleasant conversation. The big clock on the dining room bureau said seven o'clock.

Granddaddy left the table to walk about the yard and barnyard. Sometimes if he was in a hurry, he would sit on the ground and scoot down the hill, pulling his crutches along beside him. But most often, he would go up in the back field and walk in the hilltop meadow where Bossie grazed and where Uncle Byrd and Uncle Ward had planted a cornfield for him. Beyond the cornfield was the hayfield. The road to Calhoun ran along the edge of the meadow, and a gate opened from the field into the dirt road on level ground. He walked along, placing his crutches in front and swinging his good leg up to the crutches. His white hair and beard framed his Scot Irish high cheekbones and strong ruddy face, which turned this way and that as he surveyed his land. The cornfield was growing nicely, yellow-white seedy tassels waved in the gentle breeze. He continued along the path that edged his property. Brush grew up the roadside hill toward the fence at the top. The hay had been cut once in early summer, and a new crop was getting a good start. Hopefully, they could get another cutting if the weather cooperated. At the gate that opened into the road, Granddaddy paused to wipe his sweaty face. It took all his energy to make these morning excursions, but he enjoyed them immensely. He hoped the infection in his leg bones could be controlled a little longer. He stood by the gate to rest and contemplate God's blessings and to reflect on his past and future. Soon, he would start the long and difficult journey back down the road to the bottom of the hill where the lower garden grew and the horses grazed in the meadow by the creek. The barn, woodshed, and road to Byrd and Ward's would greet him upon his return. It would take him three hours to walk around this part of his hundred-acre farm.

Millie and Aunt Susie helped Grandmother clear the table and do the dishes. Millie filled the water bucket from the well pump, and soon they were ready to tackle the parlor. Curtis Lee strolled in just as they were starting to take the bed apart. He too was excited about papering the walls.

Together they carried the straw tick mattress and feather comforter into the yard to sun and air. The curtains were taken down, and Grandmother put them to soak in warm soapy water in a washtub out back. Millie and Curtis Lee got two stepladders from behind the house. Grandmother would cook the wheat paste, and Aunt Susie and the children would hang the wallpaper. They started at one corner and worked around the room. Measuring the wallpaper by holding it up to the ceiling and marking it, they took it down, cut it, applied the wheat paste on the back of the paper with a wide brush, and hung it again by rubbing it against the wall.

The children each had a stepladder, and they held the paper between them. They pressed the paper against the wall with clean rags and a soft scrub brush. The children rubbed lightly downward under Aunt Susie's direction. She smoothed the newly hung paper at the lower half while encouraging the young workers a little more to the left or a little to the right in an effort to keep it straight. It was difficult work for the two eight-year-olds, soon to be nine. But both were accustomed to work and so were thrilled and delighted with their progress as the bright cream-colored wallpaper with multicolored flicks covered the old dingy flowered one. They were very serious workers and cooperated beautifully; Aunt Susie told them often. Grandmother brought them tall glasses of sweet tea to drink when they took a rest. By eleven o'clock, they were about half done and they were sure one day would do it.

Aunt Susie said to stop while she and Grandmother prepared dinner. Granddaddy was back on the porch, and the children took their tea and joined him. He was sipping tea too and looking down the road toward the highway. The mail lay on the table beside him, and the newspaper was on his lap. The sweet smell of honeysuckle mingled with the fresh country air.

"Well, how're the paper hangers doing?" he asked cheerfully.

"OK, we're going to be done today, I think," Curtis Lee replied as he sat on the swing. Millie sat in Grandmother's chair.

"Granddaddy, tell us another story, please," Millie pleaded.

Chapter 6

When Granddaddy Met Grandmother

"Oh, I like to tell stories, all right." Granddaddy smiled. He continued to gaze down the road as though expecting someone. "But I don't know any paper hanger stories."

"We like your stories about when you were a missionary. Tell us one of those kind," Millie encouraged. "Well, I could tell you about the time I met your grandmother. Would you like that?" "Yeah!" the two children exclaimed in a chorus. "Well, sir, I was twenty-nine years old, and I had been doing missionary work for eight years. I figured it was time I settled down. So I had my eye open for a pretty lassie, you see. I had a circuit then, and one time I stayed at your grandma's house. Her dad was one of the most prominent men in the area. English gentry! He had two daughters of marriageable age. Your grandma was sixteen, a real lady, and her sister was eighteen. Well, sir, I took a shine to your grandma, as you know, and that presented a problem. When I asked her dad for her hand, he said he had to get her sister married first. I wasn't interested in her sister. I was interested in Mistie. That's your grandma, you know!" He studied the children's faces and was pleased with the interest and attention they were showing. His hazel eyes sparkled in remembrance as he stroked his white beard and mustache. His tea glass was empty, and he reached for his pipe.

"What happened next?" Millie wanted to know.

"Yeah," said Curtis Lee. "I never heard this story before."

Granddaddy lighted his pipe slowly, drawing deeply on the pipe stem until smoke clouds puffed away in the morning breeze. He was silent while he puffed on the pipe, filling the air with sweet tobacco smells. The porch was always in the shade, and almost always, a breeze stirred the ivy leaves along the porch railing. The children watched their granddaddy in fascinated silence, waiting for him to continue his storytelling.

"Well, sir, I tell you, I didn't rightly know what to do. I knew she took a shine to me too. 'Cause I could tell, you see. When you get older, you'll understand those things. Anyway, I saw her after church on the day I was to move on to the next town. I asked her if she'd like to be my wife and go away with me. She said yes if her dad gave his permission. I told her I was going on to my calling but I'd be back in a month and if she wanted to go to be ready. Then I left. Four weeks later, I came back, she was ready, we got hitched, and that's how it happened!" He slapped his leg, stamped his good foot on the porch floor, threw his head back, and laughed loudly at the surprised expressions on the children's faces.

Millie and Curtis Lee looked at each other in puzzlement, and then they laughed too. "But, Granddaddy, didn't you go a-courtin'?" Curtis Lee wanted to know.

"Nope. I knew what I wanted. She knew what she wanted and that was that."

"Grandmother was only sixteen?" Millie said in amazement.

"Ask her," Granddaddy encouraged.

Millie jumped up and ran into the kitchen where Grandmother was putting the finishing touches on dinner. "Were you really only sixteen when you married Granddaddy, and did he only see you a few times?" asked Millie of her grandmother.

"Millie, whatever your granddaddy says, that's how it was!" Grandmother would say no more.

Millie slowly turned and walked back to the porch. She looked at Curtis Lee and nodded. "She said whatever Granddaddy says is right."

"Now, what do you think? You think I'd tell you a fib?" Granddaddy's eyes were merry, and although he was trying to appear serious, there was a chuckle in his voice.

"You could be telling a tall tale," Curtis Lee decided. His dad was great at telling tall tales. Millie agreed. She had heard some of Uncle Byrd's tall tales.

"Well, sir, I could be! But I'm not!" Granddaddy roared with laughter at the seriousness of the children and their puzzled doubting expressions.

He slapped his leg, stamped his foot, and laughed and laughed until tears filled his eyes.

"I think you're teasing us." Millie laughed.

"Me too," laughed Curtis Lee.

Granddaddy pulled a handkerchief from his pocket and wiped his eyes. He had laughed so hard he was crying. "What's all this noise out here?" Grandmother wanted to know as she stood inside the porch screen door. "It's time for dinner. Come along, now."

The good mood of the morning continued through dinner. Then it was back to work in the parlor for the children and the women while Granddaddy studied his Bible and worked on his writings on the porch.

At long last, the room was papered all around; and the children, Aunt Susie, and Grandmother were pleased with the result. "We couldn't have hired anyone to do it better!" Aunt Susie declared. "Good as new, I'd say!" exclaimed Grandmother. "You both are really good workers. Thank you for your help!"

"It was fun," Millie said as she surveyed their work with pride.

"Yeah," said Curtis Lee. "What can we do tomorrow?"

"Tomorrow you and Millie can take the new horse, Boots, to the store and get some groceries. OK?" Aunt Susie said.

"Yahoo!" "Hurrah!" shouted the children. At last, they'd get to ride Boots. That would be a lot of fun. It was time for Curtis Lee to go home and begin the evening chores. Millie went with Aunt Susie to gather the eggs and feed the chickens. Then she went for Bossie and stopped to scratch the sides on one of the pigs with a stick through the fence of the pigpen. He grunted contentedly with each scratch. Afterward, she carried another load of wood up the hill from the woodpile and filled the water bucket for Grandmother. Together they carried the straw tick mattress and feather comforter back inside.

Supper was leftovers from dinner. Granddaddy usually had corn bread and milk. Millie didn't like corn bread that much, but she liked cold biscuits with butter and jelly. After supper, Aunt Susie and Millie played dominos at the dining room table while Grandmother crocheted on the porch and talked to Granddaddy. Soon it was bedtime. In bed that night, Millie asked Aunt Susie, "Did Granddaddy and Grandmother really get married without courting?"

"Yes, Millie. That's what they both say, so I guess that's how it was. Times were different then and people had to make up their minds quickly. You've heard the saying, 'If you get burned, you'll just have to sit on the blister,' well, that was how people looked at things. If things didn't work out like you expected them to, it was just too bad. That's how life is. You do the best you can and that's good enough."

"But, Aunt Susie, do you think Grandmother was sorry she did that?"

"If she was, she never complained about it. I never heard Mommy complain or criticize Poppy about anything. Not even once," reflected Aunt Susie. "She has always believed Poppy is a messenger of God and who is she to criticize him. Now, to bed with you and don't forget your prayers."

"I won't," Millie said as she knelt to pray. Aunt Susie listened from behind the folding screen and came to brush her long hair before the mirror.

Grandmother

Chapter 7

An Adventure to Remember

Curtis Lee came early the next day. Breakfast was just ending when he strolled through the door with, "Morning, everybody!"

"How's your mother and dad today, Curtis Lee?" Grandmother asked.

"Oh, they're all right. Dad went to the field and Mom went to town. So I thought I'd come on down."

"I'm glad you did, Curtis Lee. How about some breakfast?" Grandmother brought another plate and silverware.

"Thanks. Don't mind if I do. Everyone was gone when I got up. Mom left me a note, though." After Curtis Lee had eaten, he helped Millie and Aunt Susie clear the table and Millie and Grandmother do the dishes. They moved the furniture back into the parlor and took the feather comforter and straw tick mattress back outside to air. Aunt Susie and the children set up the curtain stretchers and helped stretch the clean, wet lace curtains onto the sharp nails for drying. Granddaddy went for his morning walk, and soon, it was time to go get Boots. "Come on, you two, we'll go get Boots while your grandmother makes the grocery list," Aunt Susie said. They stopped at the barn to get a lead rope.

"How will we get her to come?" Millie asked.

"I'll whistle for her," Curtis Lee replied.

"Will she come to a whistle, Aunt Susie?" Millie asked.

"I don't know, but we'll see," was the reply.

"I never get to ride horses," Millie declared. "Only mules. We have old John and Jerry, and it's fun riding them, but we don't have a saddle or anything like that. This is going to be fun!"

"Yeah!" exclaimed Curtis Lee. "You ride in the saddle, Millie, and I'll ride behind, OK?"

"Sure, that's fine with me," Millie answered. The children and Aunt Susie approached the gate to the meadow across the road where the horses grazed. Aunt Susie had an apple cut in fours in her apron pocket, but she hadn't told the children. If Boots came to Curtis Lee's whistle, then she'd give her an apple piece as a reward. If not, she'd show the apple to get her to come.

"Come on, Boots," the children called. Curtis Lee whistled his horse call. The horses in the field raised their heads and pointed their ears, alert to the sharp whistle. They turned toward the whistle and saw the people. Old Molly, Grandmother's gray mare, came toward them first then Duke, Aunt Susie's horse, followed. Boots stood still for several seconds and then she too followed the others toward the gate.

"Good, Curtis Lee!" Aunt Susie praised him. "Now, here is an apple piece for each of you to give to the horses. Which one will you give your apple to, Millie?"

Millie looked at Curtis Lee. She knew he wanted to give his to Boots, and she thought Aunt Susie would want to give a piece to Duke. "I'll give my piece to Molly," she said holding the apple quarter in her open palm. She knew how to feed a horse. She'd fed John and Jerry many times.

The horses came to the gate. "You children stay on the outside and give your apple through the fence," Aunt Susie directed. The children and Aunt Susie rubbed the horses' noses and gave them each an apple quarter from their open palms. The horses nuzzled the apple pieces, picking them up with their big lips. While they nuzzled for more, Aunt Susie slipped through the gate to Boots and slid the rope halter around her nose, over her ears, and around her neck. She offered her a second piece of apple, and Boots followed Aunt Susie out of the gate. Curtis Lee hurried to latch the gate behind her before the other horses could follow Boots out.

Aunt Susie handed the rope to Curtis Lee who patted Boots on the nose and said, "Good girl! Good girl!"

Millie patted Boots on her side and neck. Her bronze-colored hair glistened in the morning light. "She's really a pretty horse!" Millie exclaimed.

"Yes, I think she'll do well. We needed another workhorse to help with the farmwork. Old Molly can't work anymore, and Duke can't do it all by himself. Now we have Boots, and she's gentle as can be to ride." Curtis Lee led her to the barn and then he gave the rope to Millie and went in the barn to get the bridle, blanket, and saddle and put them on Boots. Aunt Susie checked the belly belt and bridle. All was in place. Saddlebags were thrown behind the saddle for the groceries. The children walked to a pile of wood to climb on for ease in mounting. Millie mounted first and sat in the saddle. Curtis Lee mounted behind her and sat on the leather strap of the saddlebags. They looked down at Aunt Susie.

"We're ready, Aunt Susie," Curtis Lee said.

"I see! Ride up to the house and tell Mommy you're ready. She'll give you the grocery list. Now, be careful. Don't hurry and stay off the highway. Keep her on the roadside. You shouldn't have any trouble."

"OK," came the chorus in reply. Millie held the bridle reins in her hand as Boots climbed the hill in a zigzag fashion with the children leaning forward. Grandmother was standing on the porch. She came to the fence and handed the grocery list to Millie. Millie looked at the paper and read, "Five pounds of sugar, one pound of coffee, one box of salt, one can Prince Albert tobacco, ten cents of candy. Thanks, Grandmother. We'll be back before long." She stuffed the paper in her jean's pocket.

"You children take your time. Don't stop anywhere and come straight back!" Grandmother directed.

"OK. Bye, Grandmother. Bye, Aunt Susie," they called. Millie guided the bronze—colored horse with the white above her hoofs down the steep hill. Both children leaned back and held on as they zigzagged down the hill, bobbing back and forth with each step. The rock-based road was much smoother than the hill. In no time, they were out of sight of the house. As Boots walked along in the July morning, the sun beat down on the children's heads and shoulders. They could see the water bubbling and gurgling in the stream that ran beside the road. "I wonder if Boots would like a drink," Millie said. "It sure is hot!"

"Yeah, it sure is! We could give her a drink in the creek. Want to?"

"OK. Where should we cross over?"

"There's a level place down the road a little way. It's too steep here, and there's too much brush." They rode on, passed the O'Brien's house beside the road. Mrs. O'Brien was working in her flowerbed. She waved to the children, and they waved back. Soon, they reached the level place in the road where the creek and the road were nearly on the same level. The road was often flooded in rainy weather and deep ruts were cut into the roadbed and slabs of bedrock were exposed. Millie guided Boots into the path used by past travelers away from the road and toward the bubbling stream. Gingerly, Boots stepped into the pebbled stream and stood there waiting. "She can't put her head down if I hold the reins," Millie said.

"Let go of it. We can get it back," Curtis Lee decided. Millie leaned forward and threw the reins over Boots's head into the water. Boots put her head down to drink, but the bit in her mouth would not let her drink. She stepped through the reins and tried again. Still she could not drink. She tried to throw her head back and try again, but the rein was between her legs.

"I'm getting scared, Curtis Lee. We better go on to the store. I don't think she's thirsty anyway. She's not even drinking."

"Yeah, I forgot about the bit in her mouth." Suddenly Boots stumbled to one knee. Her head went down, and Millie flew over Boot's head and landed in the knee-deep water. She landed face forward flat on her stomach. Crawling to her hands and knees, she stood up. "Oh my goodness! Oh my goodness!" she repeated, dripping wet. Curtis Lee, who had been thrown to the side, scrambled to his feet and grabbed the bridle strap beside Boots's nose. He guided Boots backward to step through the reins and then threw it over her head again.

"Come on! We'll be in big trouble now!" Curtis Lee shouted. He led Boots along the creek bed to a higher bank, and they mounted her again. This time, Curtis Lee sat in the saddle, and Millie sat behind. Both children were dripping wet and trembling. Although Boots may have cooled her feet, she had not been able to drink.

"How stupid! Why didn't we think about that bit?" Millie chattered nervously. "Now what are we going to do?"

"I don't know. Do you want to go back to the house?"

"No, let's go ahead slow. Maybe we'll dry out before we get to the store. It's so hot." Millie didn't want to admit to being so foolish. They would get the groceries, she decided. She hoped Mr. Dye at the store wouldn't tell her mom and get her in deep trouble.

"Mr. Dye will tell," Curtis Lee said, as if reading her thoughts. "He'll ask how we got wet. Then what will we say?"

"We'll just tell him. We wanted to give Boots a drink because it is so hot. We forgot about the bit. She fell down and so did we, but we're OK and we want the groceries." She felt in her pocket for the grocery list. It was soaking wet. If she pulled it out, maybe it would dry before they got there.

"Do you remember what Grandmother wanted?" Curtis Lee asked.

"Let's see, sugar, coffee, tobacco, and . . ."

"There was something else. Was it salt?"

"Yeah, that's it! We don't need the list. There was ten cents for candy on it too, remember?"

"But will Mr. Dye believe us without the note?"

"I think so. It goes on the bill anyway, and he knows I'm visiting 'cause I stopped there with the mail when I came over." Millie was happy again. They were slowly drying. Her short blond hair had stopped dripping, and some of the dampness was leaving her shirt and jeans.

"Anyway, it's cooler, eh?" Curtis Lee smiled. He was drying too. His freckles were dark in his tanned complexion, and his brown hair, short in a crew cut, didn't hold water at all. His thin cotton T-shirt was nearly dry. Only his jeans and tennis shoes were wet. "Maybe he'll not even notice," he reasoned.

"Yeah. Should we stop for a while, do you think, so we can dry more?"

"No, I don't think so, Millie. We better go straight to the store and back like Aunt Susie and Grandmother said. OK?"

"OK." They rode on in silence for a while. Along the road on the left was a small log cabin. Its door hung by one hinge, and there was no glass in the windows. Weeds had grown tall around the porch and sides. They looked at the abandoned house.

"Do you think there are ghosts of slaves in there?" Curtis Lee asked.

"Who said anything about that?"

"Well, I heard that was a slave house back in the olden days, and I wondered if there were any ghosts in there."

"Curtis Lee! You're just saying that to try to scare me! But I'm not afraid of ghosts. My dad said there's no such thing as ghosts, and I believe it!"

"You never really know. There could be!"

"Well, I don't believe it!" Millie insisted. As they continued on the rock-based road, the highway came into view. Cars and trucks whizzed by.

"Wonder if Boots will be spooked by the traffic?" Millie said.

"No, Aunt Susie said her other owner said she didn't pay it any mind."

"Good!" Millie felt relieved. They walked almost in the drainage ditch along the highway. The roadsides were wide, and Boots walked unconcerned with the traffic when it whizzed passed them. At the store, the children dismounted onto the store's porch and Curtis Lee held the reins as Millie went inside to get the groceries. Her list was crumpled and unreadable. She hoped Mr. Dye would believe her.

"Well, Millie! What a surprise! What happened to you, you're all wet?" Mr. Dye was behind the counter of his general store. The room was dark when Millie walked inside. It took a few minutes for her eyes to adjust to the light change. No one else was there.

"Hi, Mr. Dye. Curtis Lee and I were coming to the store on Aunt Susie's new horse, Boots, and we fell in the creek. But we're OK, and I have a list from Grandmother to put on the bill. You can't read it, but I know what it says."

"Whoa! Now start again. You fell off the horse? Are you hurt?"

"No."

"You're all right?"

"Yeah."

"Where's Curtis Lee?"

"He's outside with Boots."

Mr. Dye walked out on the porch. Curtis Lee stood beside Boots, the reins in his hand.

"Hi, Mr. Dye," he said cheerfully.

"What happened to you two anyway?"

"Oh, nothing."

"Nothing? It looks to me like you're all wet."

"Oh, just a little damp. It'll dry."

"Hump! Well, all right! Let me see your list, Millie." Mr. Dye frowned. His bushy eyebrows met together above his eyes. His bushy brown hair seemed to have a mind of its own and stood out from his head no matter how he combed it. He took the list in his hand, and Millie noticed the long brown hair on his hands and arms. She'd never paid that much attention to Mr. Dye before, but he was definitely hairy, she decided. "I can't read this!" he exclaimed.

"I know. But I can tell you what it says." Millie walked inside the store as though she came often and could get the things she needed without his help.

"All right. What is it?" Mr. Dye was over his surprise and ready to fill the order whether he could read it or not. After all, it was Reverend Boggs's new horse, and there was a list, and if Millie knew what was on it, well, he guessed it would be all right.

"One can of Prince Albert tobacco for Granddaddy, a pound of coffee, five pounds of sugar, one box of salt, and Curtis Lee and I get five cents of candy each." Mr. Dye gathered the order and made up the charge bill. Millie picked out what she wanted—two suckers, one bubble gum, and two railroad candy sticks with creamy stuff outside and chewy stuff inside. She held Boots while Curtis Lee chose his candy, and then with Mr. Dye's help, they loaded the groceries in the saddlebags. The children were off again, chewing their bubble gum and riding the horse slowly along the roadside near the drainage ditch.

"Whew! That was close! I thought for a while he wasn't going to let us get the groceries," Millie reflected.

"Yeah. He's nosy as all get out! He thinks he should know everybody's business," Curtis Lee said between gum bubbles. He was riding in front again, and Millie didn't mind. "Hm! Hm!" Curtis Lee grunted pointing to his gum bubble that was nearly as big as his face.

"Yeah, I see it. Wow! That's big. You better watch it, though. You might get it all over you."

Curtis Lee sucked the air back out slowly and pulled the collapsed bubble away from his face with two fingers. "Did you see that? That was really big!" he exclaimed. They talked and ate their candy as Boots ambled along. The reins lay on the saddle horn, and the children laughed and played games, pretending they were Lewis and Clark as they rode back to the house. By the time they reached the porch, they were only slightly damp. Aunt Susie unloaded the groceries from the saddlebags, and the children took Boots back to the barn. They removed the saddle and took her back to the field. Then they told Aunt Susie about their adventure, one the children would both long remember.

Chapter 8

Canning Beans

Thursday morning, Millie was supposed to help Aunt Susie pick green beans for canning while Grandmother washed the jars. Aunt Susie wore her sunbonnet, long dress with apron, garden shoes, and carried her garden basket over her arm. Millie was barefoot with her jeans rolled up to her knees. She carried a small basket and lugged two bushel baskets, one inside the other. Aunt Susie limped from the arthritis in her hip as they slowly made their way down the steep rocky hill to the garden. The mist hung heavy over the valley garden, and the sun was a white ball in the misty sky to the east. The weeds and grasses were wet with the morning dew. Crows noisily called to one another from the treetops on Bailey's hill. Perhaps they had found an unfortunate owl. "It's going to be a hot one today, Millie," Aunt Susie declared. "When the mist stays in the valley this late in the morning, it's a sure sign." She lifted the top wire from the fence post that held the wire gate upright and pulled it back so they could step through. Millie threw over her small basket and then lifted one bushel basket at a time to Aunt Susie who tossed them into the garden just inside the gate. Aunt Susie replaced the wire on the post and turned to Millie. "We'll start at this end of the bean patch and only pick the full ones. The little ones we'll leave for another day. See. Watch me pick these here." Aunt Susie gently lifted the bean vine to reveal the cluster of long green beans hanging underneath. "See these little ones here? We'll not pick them, only the bigger and longer ones." She pinched off the larger beans, placed them in her basket, and replaced the bean vine so carefully that it seemed to have never been touched. "You pick that row and I'll pick this one," Aunt Susie said.

Millie carefully lifted the bean vine as she had seen Aunt Susie do, and the bean picking began. It took them three hours to go over the patch, and when they were done, they had filled the two bushel baskets as well as Aunt Susie's garden basket. The mist had been burned away by the hot sunshine that dried the plants. Millie's head and back felt hot, and sweat ran down the sides of her face along her hairline and on her forehead into her eyes. She wiped her eyes and face with her T-shirt tail. She looked at Aunt Susie's face, which was flushed red from the heat and bending over along the rows of beans.

"Millie, you should have a hat on. You might get heatstroke. Just look how hot you are!"

"I'm OK, Aunt Susie, but how are you? Are you OK?"

"Yes, thank goodness, we're done. Can you help me move these baskets to the shade? Uncle Byrd will be here any minute, and he will carry them to the house for us. We'll just take the ones that are in the garden basket." Aunt Susie and Millie dragged the bushel baskets to a shady place and then Aunt Susie picked some ears of corn, tomatoes, and cucumbers for dinner before they left the garden.

Granddaddy was deep in thought in his chair on the porch and never even looked up as Aunt Susie and Millie silently trudged up the hill and around the house to the back door. Grandmother was at the pump getting water. "Well, it's about time you two got back! I was about ready to yell for you. Look how hot you are! Susie! Get out of that sun before you're sick!" Grandmother demanded in a stern voice. She brought a chair from the house and put it in the shade. She took the vegetables and placed them on the outside table. Millie collapsed in the cool shaded grass by the house. She could feel the heat seem to rise from her face and head. She closed her eyes and felt the weariness leave her body and thought the magic cool carpet of grass was driving it away. When she opened her eyes, Aunt Susie was sitting in the shade, stringing beans. She had changed her clothes and looked fresh if still a little flushed from the heat.

"Millie, are you all right?" Aunt Susie asked.

"I'm OK. I must have fallen asleep."

"I'd say you did! You are certainly a good little worker, Millie. You stayed right with me all morning. Now, you go freshen up. Grandmother has some news for you, I think," Aunt Susie snipped and snapped the green beans as she talked.

Millie jumped up and ran into the house, banging the kitchen screen door behind her. "Mercy!" exclaimed Grandmother as she turned from the stove.

"Grandmother! Aunt Susie said you have news for me!"

"Yes, Mary and Bob are coming tomorrow. We got a letter in the mail today." "Oh boy! That's great! I can hardly wait! What time are they coming? Where's Curtis Lee? Is he coming? How long are they going to stay?"

"Millie, slow down! Aunt Marie will be here in the morning, and the children are going to stay until Sunday. Curtis Lee will be here tomorrow too. He had work at home to do today. Now, you go freshen up 'cause dinner is almost ready."

The afternoon and evening was spent in stringing and breaking green beans, washing them, stuffing them in quart canning jars, and carrying them into the cellar. The next day, a big washtub of water with old rags on the bottom would be placed over an outside fire and the jars of beans would be placed on the rags in the tub and boiled until thoroughly cooked. But that would be tomorrow. And tomorrow, Millie's first cousins, Mary and Bob, would come. They were Millie and Curtis Lee's age, and they always had great fun together.

Chapter 9

A Visit to Curtis Lee's

Millie was up early the next day, but not before Aunt Susie, Grandmother, or Granddaddy. When Millie came downstairs, she found Granddaddy in his chair beside the living room window, his Bible on his lap. Grandmother was in the kitchen, and Aunt Susie was milking under the apple tree. Millie hurried to the outhouse and then promptly began her chore of carrying wood. It would take a lot of wood to cook the beans on the open fire. She made several trips down and up the hill, carrying wood sticks from the woodpile to the open fireplace outside the yard fence.

After breakfast, she carried more wood, pumped water and filled the washtub for canning, helped Aunt Susie gather vegetables from the garden for dinner, and all the time watched and listened for Mary and Bob. Millie wanted to have all the chores done before her cousins came so they could play.

Granddaddy started his morning walk as soon as breakfast was over. He wanted to be back on the porch before his daughter and her family came. By midmorning, the beans were on to cook, and Millie was on the porch talking to Granddaddy when Aunt Marie and Uncle Herb's Chevy pulled up at the bottom of the hill. Mary, a chubby blonde with a sunny disposition, hopped out first with her grocery bag of clothes in hand and scurried up the hill. "Grandmother! Aunt Susie! Aunt Marie's here!" Millie shouted as she scampered down the porch steps and down the hill to meet Mary. Bob, a more serious child, stood beside the car, looking toward the house. He was thin and tall for his nine years with brown hair, a round face, and clear brown eyes. He smiled at the ridiculous scene before him as Millie and Mary hugged each other and jumped up and down on the side of the hill. Soon, he too was climbing the hill with his sack of clothes. "Hi, Millie," was all he said, but his eyes twinkled like Granddaddy's and Millie knew they were going to have a good time.

Soon, all the hugs and kisses were exchanged, and Mary and Bob had deposited their sacks of clothes in the spare bedroom upstairs. Then the children were off to Curtis Lee's house. The dirt road that led to Curtis Lee's was hard packed in some places and deeply rutted in others. The children walked on top of the ruts, staying in the narrow jeep tracks made by Uncle Ward's jeep. As they walked, the children talked. "Let's see if Curtis Lee can bring Sam and if we can go to the Pyramids," Millie suggested. "I haven't had a chance to go up there yet."

"Yeah!" Mary agreed. "We can play cowboys and Indians."

"Wonder if Sam's there? What if he's not? We can't go without a dog, you know," Bob cautioned. He hated snakes.

"We could still go, maybe. Curtis Lee might take one of Uncle Byrd's foxhounds," Mary suggested as she picked up a stick from along the edge of the road that ran beside the creek and whacked weeds as they walked.

"Uncle Byrd wouldn't let us. He says his foxhounds are not pets," Bob insisted. He was looking for touch-me-nots to touch. The delicate wildflower would unfold in a sudden burst if the bud were just right. Millie looked for a good walking stick to lean on.

They passed the steep road to the left that went to the point where Uncle Ward lived. "Let's go see Uncle Ward and Aunt Irene. They have a rope swing with an old tire tied to it, and it's fun to play on." Millie had found a good solid stick. She leaned on it for a crutch and walked with one stiff leg.

"They have a rain barrel and an open well with a bucket too." Bob looked back toward the rocky road. It was like going back in time when he came to Granddaddy's farm. It was no time at all until the children were at Uncle Byrd and Aunt Hallie's where Curtis Lee and Kenneth Blaine lived. They crossed the field and started up the hill to the knoll on which the white two-story farmhouse stood. To the right at the base of the knoll sat a large gray barn with various wire fences connected to it and many wire pens. Suddenly, terrible growls and barks came from the front of the barn. Six foxhounds ran to the end of their tether, jumped on the wooden slates piled there, and barked and growled loudly.

The children stopped and stared at the dogs. Could they get loose? No, probably not. Slowly they continued toward the house as the dogs' barking became wilder and more fearful. Curtis Lee came from the side of the house with Sam at his heels. "Come on up!" he yelled. "They can't get you!" The dogs became quiet and disappeared into the barn. In his hand, Curtis Lee held a paintbrush with dark green paint on the bristles.

"What are you painting?" Bob asked.

"Mom wanted me to paint the washstand today before I went to Granddaddy's. I didn't think you all would be here this early. Come around back and see it. I'm almost done."

The children followed Curtis Lee around the side of the house to the covered cement porch and the apple tree. Standing on newspaper under the apple tree was a homemade square table that was used as an outdoor washstand. Curtis Lee had painted the legs and bottom shelf. Only the top, sides, and side rod that held the towel was left to do. He went back to covering the old chipped white paint with the forest green. Sam sniffed everyone's legs, and then satisfied with pats and petting, he went to lie in the shade of the house in Aunt Hallie's bed of daylilies. Behind the cellar loft, the sheep grazed about the hillside. Millie watched the sheep. "I wish I had a pet lamb," she said longingly.

"Can we play with the lambs, Curtis Lee?" Mary wanted to know.

"We don't have any pet lambs now. They're all wild. Dad said not to make pets of them 'cause they're a nuisance when they get older."

"I wish I had a pet lamb," Millie repeated. "My dad doesn't like sheep. He says sheep and cattle don't mix."

"I bet if Uncle Byrd gave you a lamb, your dad would let you keep it while it's little," Bob speculated. "Maybe you could sell it later and make some money."

"Yeah, I could learn to shear it and sell the wool and everything!" Millie exclaimed.

"Well, I don't know, Millie," Mary said doubtfully. "Who would teach you how and take the wool to market and all that stuff. Remember, your dad doesn't like sheep."

"Curtis Lee could teach me, couldn't you, Curtis Lee?" Millie asked as Curtis Lee cleaned his brush and put away the paint.

"Sure, only you don't even have any sheep yet, Millie," Curtis Lee reminded her.

"I know. Oh well, I can dream, can't I?" Millie said lightly.

Chapter 10

Unusual Pets

"Want to go up to Smith's?" Curtis Lee asked. "They've got a pet raccoon and a pet groundhog. Bill found the baby raccoon after the mother was caught in a trap and took it home. It's just like a cat or a dog. It follows you around and makes little clicking sounds." He had finished painting the washstand and cleaned his brush. He was ready to do something.

"Where'd they get the groundhog?" Bob wanted to know.

"Mr. Smith was groundhog hunting and killed the mother in a cornfield. He found the baby in a hole and brought it home. The raccoon and groundhog both live under the porch."

The children followed the cow path around the hillside and through the field to Smith's farm at the head of the hollow where two hills came together into a green meadow valley. "Wonder if Mrs. Smith will talk about us?" Millie asked Mary.

"Probably, she always has to say something," Mary replied.

An old unpainted two-story house with a porch all around stood on stone posts before the sloping hillsides. Smaller shacks and shanties served as animal shelters. Dogs, pigs, and chickens strayed around the house in the grass. In the meadow to the left grazed a cow and calf. On the briary hillside above the house were two goats and several sheep. There were no fences. As the children approached, a foxhound, a rabbit dog, and a sheep dog began barking and running back and forth in front of the porch. Mrs. Smith appeared at the screen door and then came onto the porch and down the front steps to quiet the dogs and call to the children. "Is that you, Curtis Lee?"

"Yes, Mrs. Smith. We came to see your pet raccoon and groundhog," Curtis Lee called back. The children began to run as they came nearer. Mrs. Smith wiped her hands on her apron and extended her arms to welcome the girls.

"Well, if it's not little Millie and Mary! I declare, Millie, you are skinnier than a string bean and, Mary, you're as round as a little butterball! And how are you, Bob?"

The children smiled and exchanged greetings and answered Mrs. Smith's questions about the family. Then she told the children to make themselves at home. A piglet came grunting from behind the house to see what the noise was about. Curtis Lee looked under the porch. "You'll have to just look around for Little Maskman. That's what we call the raccoon. Groundhog's probably under the porch. I'll get you an apple. Maybe they'll come out for something to eat." Mrs. Smith disappeared inside the house and was back out again with a big juicy apple for each child.

"Will the dogs scare them away?" asked Bob.

"They've gotten used to them and don't pay them no mind," Mrs. Smith replied. "I've got work to do, but you children make yourselves at home and give your grandma and aunt Susie my best." With that, Mrs. Smith disappeared again, and the children were left to search for the unusual pets by themselves.

Curtis Lee crawled under the porch steps and called, "Here, Little Maskman!" but he could only see darkness. He held out his apple and called again. Still no raccoon or groundhog could be seen.

Piglet followed Millie, grunting and rubbing against her leg. "You want to be petted, don't you, Piglet? Here, do you want a bite of my apple?" She bit off a piece of apple and placed it in her hand. Piglet nuzzled in her outstretched hand and took a bite of the apple, grunting happily. Millie rubbed his head and his back. He fell over on his side and looked up at her as if to say he was ready. Millie knew what Piglet wanted. She picked up a stick and gently scratched his side and belly with a back-and-forth motion. Piglet grunted contentedly.

Bob and Mary were eating their apples and looking for Little Maskman by the woodpile. They called, "Come here, Little Maskman!" A large orange tomcat came walking lazily from behind the woodpile. He stopped to stretch and yawn. Behind came what first looked like another big cat, but with a second look, the children realized it was Little Maskman. A little black mask was around his little beady eyes, and his pointy ears stood up as he came toward them. His ringed bushy tail followed him and seemed almost as big as his body. He was not one bit afraid but came right up to the children, sat on his hind legs with his little fingered hands in the air, and chattered at them. Mary handed him a piece of apple, which he took in his little fingers and ate with little tiny bites. The children watched in fascination. "Oh, he's so cute!" Mary exclaimed. "Wonder if he'll let me hold him?"

"Better not," Bob advised. Mary continued to feed Little Maskman apple pieces as he chattered at her. Little Groundhog never came out, and finally, the children started back along the cow path toward home. They didn't want to be late for dinner.

After dinner was over and Aunt Marie and Uncle Herb had left, the children were off again. They went up the dry creek bed searching for treasures, into the woods to swing on the hanging wild grapevine, up to the pyramids with Sam to play cops and robbers and then wild Indians and the cavalry. Soon, the sun was low and close to the hilltops. Long shadows fell across the valley. Curtis Lee and Sam hurried home to do the chores; and Millie, Mary, and Bob returned to Grandmother's house.

After the evening chores were done and they had eaten a light supper, Mary, Millie, and Bob played hide-and-seek in the semidarkness where a tree or bush could effectively hide a player. Granddaddy's pipe smoke drifted on the evening air and mingled with the honeysuckle. Grandmother and Aunt Susie talked quietly on the porch. Night sounds were all about, and when it was too dark to continue playing outside, a game of dominos was played at the dining room table in the light of the oil lamp. Aunt Susie made popcorn for a bedtime snack, and the happy children went to bed, excited about the prospects of tomorrow. Millie and Mary slept with Aunt Susie, and Bob slept in the spare room.

Chapter 11

Canning Corn and Playing Church

When Millie and Mary awoke, Aunt Susie was gone from the bed. They spied her through the window standing by the apple tree preparing to milk old Bossie. Mary peeked in the spare bedroom, but Bob was gone, and his bed was already made. The girls hurriedly dressed, straightened the bedroom, and scurried down the steep narrow stairs to the living room. Granddaddy was sitting in his chair by the window. "Morning, Granddaddy!" they called as they hurried by. "Morning, Grandmother!" Hickory-smoked ham frying in the pan on the woodburning cookstove sent an aroma through the early morning air that was unforgettable. "Grandmother! That smells delicious!" Millie declared, stopping to sniff the air. Grandmother, in her long dress and brightly flowered bibbed apron, smiled proudly as she turned the ham slices in the frying pan.

Bob was carrying an armload of wood up the hill in the morning mist as the girls hurried to the outhouse. They returned to help him. Then they washed their faces and hands, pumped water for the hot-water tank in the stove and the cold-water bucket on the kitchen counter. Aunt Susie and Grandmother planned to can corn. That meant gathering corn from the garden, shucking and silking it, carrying it up the hill, cutting it off the cob, placing it in canning jars, and cooking it on the open fire as they had cooked the beans.

It was a hearty breakfast, which everyone enjoyed, and then the children helped clear the table and carry the jars to be washed from the cellar. Grandmother would wash the jars while Aunt Susie and the children prepared the corn. The clock on the dining room bureau said seven o'clock.

Aunt Susie and the children gathered their baskets, pans, and knives for cutting out bad places. Then the children watched while Aunt Susie put on her sunbonnet, long-sleeved shirt, and garden shoes. Granddaddy was in the yard preparing to take his morning walk to the upper field. At last, Aunt Susie was ready and down the rocky hill they went, chattering and laughing as only eight—and nine-year-old children do.

Soon, a basket of corn was pulled and carried to the barnyard gate beside the woodpile at the bottom of the hill. Mary and Millie began shucking and silking (pulling the outside cover and silk off the ears) while Bob continued to help Aunt Susie pull the ready ears from the stalks. The little girls giggled, told tales and jokes, made plans, and had a great visit as they worked. Just when they thought they were getting ahead, Bob dumped another batch on the ground where the others had been. When the girls had a pan full of freshly cleaned corn, they carried it up the hill to Grandmother who cut the corn off the ears.

When the children began working, the cool mist was all about, but the hot sun soon burned the mist away and it boiled down on the workers. The girls moved their work area to the shade of the huge beech tree that grew near the creek bank. By midmorning, the corn was gathered and Aunt Susie, Bob, Mary and Millie were all shucking and silking. Five bushels of corn ears were cleaned and carried to the house.

Aunt Susie and Grandmother praised the good workers. The children drank some cool well water and sat on the porch to relax and talk with Granddaddy while dinner was being prepared. Afternoon was the children's time to play, and after a filling dinner, they were off to see Curtis Lee.

Curtis Lee had been helping his mother can corn too. But when the children came, he was allowed to stop and play. They lay on the cool grass under the big oak tree in Curtis Lee's yard and talked. It was too hot to do much, and the children were not in the mood to go visit anyone. "We can play church," Mary suggested.

"Who will be the preacher?" Millie asked.

"Bob can be the preacher," Curtis Lee suggested. "He'll be a good one."

"OK," Bob agreed. "Let's have a revival and baptize people."

"Yeah!" they all agreed. Curtis Lee brought a stool for Bob to stand on to preach. They indicated the river area in a yellow-green grassy area of the yard. Bob stood on the stool and looked at his congregation of three. He recalled many revivals he had attended with his parents. He began with a quote of scripture. The children were required to learn a new verse each week for Sunday school so that was no problem for Bob. He recited the Twenty-third Psalm. Curtis Lee obliged with many "amens" during the recitation.

"Are you saved?" Bob asked.

"Yes, sir!" the others responded.

"Then let's go baptize you sinners so the world can see you love the Lord!"

"No!" protested Millie. "We haven't sung any songs yet."

"OK. What do you want to sing?" asked Bob.

"Let's sing, 'Shall We Gather at the River.'" The small group sang as they walked to the yellow-green grassy spot and stopped along the edge while Preacher Bob waded into the pretend water, raised his eyes to the heavens, and prayed for God to receive the sinners. Millie was first. Brother Curtis Lee helped Preacher Bob as Sister Millie waded into the pretend water with a solemn expression of anticipation.

"Don't you drop me!" she whispered. Then she made her body stiff and held her nose.

Preacher Bob held his hand above her head and was silent for a few seconds. Then he said loudly, "I now baptize you in the name of the Father, Son, and Holy Ghost," and together, Bob and Curtis Lee slowly lowered Millie's stiff body backward toward the ground and back up again.

"Praise God!" shouted Mary. Millie pretended to wipe her face, and she smiled broadly.

"Praise God!" they all shouted.

"My turn," Mary announced. The process was repeated. Curtis Lee took his turn to go down with Millie and Bob holding him. Then Millie and Mary had another turn before the playacting ended. Soon, it was time to go back to Grandmother's and help with the evening chores. It was bath night too.

In 1943 on a farm in West Virginia, daily baths were not common. Most families took their baths on Saturday night and took "sponge baths" or washed from a pan of water the rest of the week. Therefore, Saturday was bath night at Grandmother Boggs's so after a light supper, a washtub was brought into the kitchen for baths. Aunt Susie filled the tub for the girls first. They got their pajamas, and after their kitchen bath, they played dominos with Aunt Susie. Bob helped carry out the girls' bathwater and fixed his. Then after his bath, it was off to bed for the children. In bed, the girls could hear Aunt Susie and Grandmother in the kitchen below preparing baths for themselves and Granddaddy.

Millie and Mary whispered in the darkness, telling ghost stories and tall tales between giggles and yawns until they fell asleep.

Aunt Susie

Chapter 12

Ancestors

Sunday was church day. The children had brought their church clothes to go with Aunt Susie. They walked across the hill, taking the shortcut through Bailey's farm, following the cow paths up one hill and down the other to the farm road, and on the public road that led to the small country nondenominational church. "Did you know your great-great-grandfather donated the land for the church?" Aunt Susie asked the children as they walked.

"No, I didn't know that!" Millie exclaimed. "Gee! Did he own all this land here once?"

"Yes, Millie. Your great-great-great-grandfather, John Boggs, was a well-to-do gentleman farmer. He owned thousands of acres of land and even had slaves before the civil war. He gave each of his children a portion of the land, and this was a part of your great-great-grandfather's portion. Then he divided his land up among his children, and that's where it is today."

"Where did our great-great-great-grandfather get all that land to start with?" Bob asked as they followed Aunt Susie along the cow path made by animals.

"Well, it's a long story, Bob. Your ancestors and mine were brave people. John Boggs, who was born in Ireland, came to this country as a small child. He fought bravely in the American Revolution with the Virginia Rifleman and the Indian wars too. He first lived in southern Virginia and was a cattleman and tobacco farmer. He later moved to what is now West

Virginia and bought eight thousand acres of land. When he moved, he had slaves and after the civil war, they became free but continued to live with the family for a while. Your great-grandfather inherited land from his father that included this area here. Then your grandfather, that's Poppy, inherited his portion. That's where we live today." Aunt Susie kept to the path and the children followed her, trailing in narrow places, running to catch up, and walking beside her in level places. Soon, they would be on the farm road where wagon wheels and farm trucks traveled.

"I wish I lived in pioneer days, don't you, Mary?" Millie exclaimed. "Think of it! Indians and wild animals everywhere!"

"You're crazy, Millie!" Mary declared. "I wouldn't like it, I know! I'd be scared all the time!"

"No, you wouldn't," Bob said confidently. "People had guns, and everyone knew how to shoot. Men went hunting for their food and trapped animals and everything." He recalled his history lesson at school and the exciting stories of pioneer days.

"Well, Mary, I think you would not be any more scared then than you are now 'cause you wouldn't know any other kind of life. You'd feel safe unless something scared you, and you'd always be kept close to your family. Remember this, children, your family is more important than anything. They'll take care of you when no one else will," Aunt Susie said. She had never married and had spent her life caring for her nine brothers and sisters, her mother, and her crippled father. Millie remembered when Aunt Susie had stayed with her family when Mom was in the hospital.

"Aunt Susie, you really do help your family. We'll remember," Millie reassured her.

Chapter 13

The Country Church

The white country church with its tall bell steeple was before them across the highway. Cars were parked in front and along the side of the road. People walked slowly toward the church door dressed in their Sunday best. Aunt Susie and the girls stopped to look at each other to see if they remained presentable after their mile-and-a-half walk across Bailey's farm. They decided they did. Bob was staring into the water of Duck Creek for minnows, perch, or bass.

Aunt Susie greeted her neighbors and friends of many years, exchanging family news and inquiring as to the health of others. Millie, Mary, and Bob filed into a pew about midway to the front with Aunt Susie slowly coming down the aisle shaking hands and exchanging greetings. The children looked around but couldn't see anyone they knew.

The front of the church was elevated with a podium in the center on which lay an open Bible. Chairs with high backs stood along the walls behind the podium, and a huge picture of Jesus with his disciples hung in the center above and behind the podium. A sturdy piano stood to the right of the podium below the elevation, and Mrs. McGlothlin sat on the piano bench and arranged her music book.

Tall steeple-shaped windows lined both sides of the church, and they were opened as far as they would go. A gentle breeze drifted through, and the sounds of cars passing on the highway were very distracting. It was a small church with only two columns of handmade wooden pews arranged in rows with an aisle up the middle and sides. Drapery rods crisscrossed close to the ceiling, and long draperies hung along the walls in four locations. When pulled, they divided the church pews into four class areas—children, teens, men and women, and old people. Each class had a teacher with church literature.

Mr. McGlothlin rose from his pew in front to stand beside Mrs. McGlothlin at the piano. "For our first hymn, turn to page 15. We'll sing all four verses. Everyone stand!" he announced. Mrs. McGlothlin played the piano and although slightly off-key, no greater gusto or enthusiasm could be found anywhere than was rendered in praise of the Lord from that little country church. After prayers, announcements, birthdays, and anniversaries, it was time for classes. The draperies were drawn, and each group moved to their assigned location. The children were up front so Mary, Millie, and Bob made their way to sit on the front pew with four other children sitting stiffly in their Sunday best. Mrs. Miller was their teacher, and she had little picture cards of Jesus with writing on the back to give each child. Each child was asked to say a Bible verse and explain what it meant. Then Mrs. Miller told a story about Jesus, said a short prayer, gave each child a candy stick, and took them outside under a shade tree to play a game of drop the handkerchief.

Drop the handkerchief was a fun game. Everyone sat in a circle. One person walked around the outside of the circle with a handkerchief and after going around once, dropped the handkerchief behind a sitting child. Without looking behind, the chosen child must jump up, grab the handkerchief, and tag the runner before he/she could get back to their seat. If the runner got to their seat before being tagged, it was their turn again. But if caught, it was the other person's turn to drop the handkerchief. Millie sat still and looked straight ahead. Out of the corner of her eye, she could see the walker coming her way. Would she be chosen? No, the walker passed her by and chose another, but as the game was played, each child had a turn to drop the handkerchief. It was fun, Millie thought.

Soon, it was time for the worship service called church. The steeple bell rang its dong, dong, dong, and more people began to arrive. It was preaching Sunday, and Preacher Babcock would give the sermon. Aunt Susie appeared at the door, beckoning the children to her. They sat near the front again. Aunt Susie said that was best. Millie looked at her watch she had gotten for her birthday—ten thirty. Would church start on time?

She stood up and turned around. People were still coming in. She hoped the service would start soon. It was somewhat hot and stuffy in the little church even though the windows were open, and a slight breeze brought a whiff of fresh air from time to time. Three men and a lady filled the tall chairs at the back of the podium beneath the picture of Jesus and his disciples. They were the Gospel Quartet. Preacher Babcock was seated in the first chair on the left. Mrs. McGlothlin was seated at the piano. All seemed ready, but people were still arriving so they waited. People brought out their paper fans and fanned themselves as they talked quietly.

Finally, Preacher Babcock arose to face a full church congregation and the service began with prayer, continued with singing, announcements, with the Gospel Quartet singing three songs, a reading of the scripture, and the sermon. Preacher Babcock was a hell-and-brimstone type of preacher who called all sinners to repent and be saved. He warned of the consequences of evil ways and the rewards of godliness. He called for confessions of wrongdoing and testimonies of God's grace so that the church community could pray for all those in need. A few brave souls stood to confess to minor errors in transgressions and to request for prayers for ailing bodies or to report times of trials. All unsaved souls were called to repent during the singing of the last hymn before it was too late, but no one came forward. Millie looked at her watch. It was twelve noon. No wonder she felt restless and hungry. Although she liked church and knew it was very important, she was glad the service was over and they could go home.

It was a general time for soul cleansing even as Saturday night was a time for cleansing of the body, an inspired Aunt Susie proclaimed on the way home. "Remember, children, cleanliness is next to godliness and we must be clean in the spirit as well as the body," she told them.

Grandmother had a chicken-and-dumplings dinner ready, and Aunt Marie and Uncle Herb had arrived when Aunt Susie and the children returned from church. At the table, Grandmother wanted to know about church—who was there, what was the news, what was the sermon. Aunt Susie had much to tell, but the children only spoke when asked. They were anxious to get outside and play before Mary and Bob had to leave.

As the hot, sticky Sunday afternoon grew into evening and long shadows fell across the valley, clouds gathered and thunder rumbled in the distance. The grown-ups sat on the porch and talked. Under the shade of the huge beech tree near the barn, the children waded barefoot in the shallow water puddles of the creek, searching for crawl crabs and mudpuppies. Aunt Marie called from the porch for Mary and Bob to come. It was time to go home. Millie knew her visit was ending too. Tomorrow she would catch a ride with Uncle Ward, the mailman, to go home. She had had a great time!